1812
Caroline's
SECRET MESSAGE

By KATHLEEN ERNST

ILLUSTRATIONS ROBERT PAPP

VIGNETTES LISA PAPP

★ American Girl®

THE AMERICAN GIRLS

1764   **KAYA**, an adventurous Nez Perce girl whose deep love for horses and respect for nature nourish her spirit

1774   **FELICITY**, a spunky, spritely colonial girl, full of energy and independence

1812   **CAROLINE**, a daring, self-reliant girl who learns to steer a steady course amid the challenges of war

1824   **JOSEFINA**, a Hispanic girl whose heart and hopes are as big as the New Mexico sky

1853   **CÉCILE AND MARIE-GRACE**, two girls whose friendship helps them—and New Orleans— survive terrible times

1854   **KIRSTEN**, a pioneer girl of strength and spirit who settles on the frontier

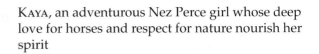

1864 ADDY, a courageous girl determined to be free in the midst of the Civil War

1904 SAMANTHA, a bright Victorian beauty, an orphan raised by her wealthy grandmother

1914 REBECCA, a lively girl with dramatic flair growing up in New York City

1934 KIT, a clever, resourceful girl facing the Great Depression with spirit and determination

1944 MOLLY, who schemes and dreams on the home front during World War Two

1974  JULIE, a fun-loving girl from San Francisco who faces big changes—and creates a few of her own

Published by American Girl Publishing
Copyright © 2012 by American Girl

Questions or comments? Call 1-800-845-0005, visit **americangirl.com**,
or write to Customer Service, American Girl, 8400 Fairway Place,
Middleton, WI 53562-0497.

Printed in China
12 13 14 15 16 17 LEO 10 9 8 7 6 5 4 3 2 1

All American Girl marks, Caroline™, and Caroline Abbott™
are trademarks of American Girl.

Deep appreciation to Constance Barone, Director, Sackets Harbor Battlefield
State Historic Site; Dianne Graves, historian; James Spurr, historian and First Officer,
Friends Good Will, Michigan Maritime Museum; and Stephen Wallace, former Interpretive
Programs Assistant, Sackets Harbor Battlefield State Historic Site.

PICTURE CREDITS
The following individuals and organizations have generously given permission to reprint
images contained in "Looking Back": p. 79—*The Girl I Left Behind Me,* 1880 (oil on canvas) by
Charles Green (1840–98), New Walk Museum & Art Gallery, Leicester, UK/Photo © Leicester
Arts & Museums/The Bridgeman Art Library, detail; pp. 80–81—*Crowninshield's Wharf,*
1806, by George Ropes, Jr., photograph courtesy of the Peabody Essex Museum, catalog no.
M3459, detail (wharf); Anne S.K. Brown Military Collection, Brown University Library, detail
(soldiers attacking); Picture Collection, The New York Public Library, Astor, Lenox and Tilden
Foundations, detail (refugees); pp. 82–83—*The Girl I Left Behind Me,* 1880 (oil on canvas) by
Charles Green (1840–98), New Walk Museum & Art Gallery, Leicester, UK/Photo © Leicester
Arts & Museums/The Bridgeman Art Library; North Wind Picture Archives (rider); © Ackworth
School, detail (mother and daughter sewing); pp. 84–85—Picture Collection, The New York
Public Library, Astor, Lenox and Tilden Foundations, detail (Fanny Doyle);
Wisconsin Historical Society, Image #2153 (map sampler).

Cataloging-in-Publication Data available from the Library of Congress

FOR MY PARENTS,
WHO FILLED OUR HOME
WITH BOOKS

Caroline Abbott is growing up in Sackets Harbor, New York, right on the shore of Lake Ontario. Just across the lake is the British colony of *Upper Canada*.

In 1812, the nation of Canada didn't exist yet. Instead, the lands north of the Great Lakes were still a collection of British colonies. Today, Upper Canada is the Canadian province of Ontario.

In Caroline's time, there was a colony called *Lower Canada*, too. It stretched from Upper Canada eastward to the Atlantic Ocean. Today, it's the province of Quebec.

TABLE OF CONTENTS

CAROLINE'S FAMILY AND FRIENDS

CAROLINE'S FAMILY

PAPA
*Caroline's father,
a fine shipbuilder
who is being held in
a British prison*

MAMA
*Caroline's mother, a firm
but understanding woman*

CAROLINE
*A daring girl who wants
to be captain of her
own ship one day*

GRANDMOTHER
*Mama's widowed mother,
who makes her home with the
Abbott family*

LYDIA
*Caroline's eleven-year-old
cousin and good friend, who
lives in Upper Canada*

SETH
*A young post walker who
delivers mail to nearby
farms and villages*

RHONDA
HATHAWAY
*A twelve-year-old girl
from the big city of
Albany who boards at
the Abbotts' house*

UNCLE AARON &
AUNT MARTHA
*Caroline's uncle and aunt,
who settled in Upper Canada
a few years earlier*

MR. TATE
*The chief carpenter at
Abbott's and a friend
of Caroline's family*

HOME AGAIN

 Caroline Abbott shivered as she kicked
the kitchen door closed behind her.
She eased a muddy pumpkin to the
floor. "Here's one to cook today, fresh from the
garden," she told Grandmother. "I'll put the rest in
the root cellar."

"Good," Grandmother said. "My bones tell me
that a hard freeze is coming." From her chair near
the fire, she leaned forward to stir the bean pot.

Caroline rubbed her hands on her apron. *It's
bad enough that we're fighting the British,* she thought.
Now the coming winter made her feel as if a second
enemy was creeping close, ready to pounce.

"Perhaps Mama can stay home from the shipyard

tomorrow," she said, "and help us handle the harvest."

"It's not easy for your mother to manage the shipyard without your father," Grandmother said. Soldiers were holding Caroline's papa and her cousin Oliver prisoner across Lake Ontario in the British colony of Upper Canada. Grandmother added, "Back during the Revolutionary War, I held my farm together with your mama's help. You and I can manage here now."

"Of course we can," Caroline said quickly. She didn't want Grandmother to think she was complaining! "I'll get back to work."

Caroline snugged her shawl against the October chill and went back to the muddy garden. She could see her neighbor, Mrs. Shaw, busy in her garden, too. The weather had been growing steadily colder, and everyone was busy with harvest chores.

After hauling the pumpkins to the root cellar, Caroline grabbed a shovel. *Next, the potatoes,* she thought. She sat the shovel upright beside the mound of earth that held the first potato plant. Then she jumped onto the blade edge with both feet.

As she teetered there, using her weight to shove the blade beneath the buried potatoes, a whistle shrilled behind her. She lost her balance and tumbled to the ground. "Ow!"

"Oh, pardon me!" Her friend Seth Whittleslee leaned on the garden gate. His eyes danced with mischief. "Did I startle you?"

Caroline scrambled to her feet, slapping at the mud on her skirt. "Seth, that was unkind," she scolded. She couldn't stay annoyed with her good friend, though. His visits were too rare.

"Can you stay for supper?" she added hopefully. With Papa gone, having Seth at the table would make the meal seem less lonely.

"You're inviting me to stay for supper?" Seth asked, pretending to be surprised. "Why, how very kind of you."

Caroline snorted. Seth was the local post walker, tramping far from the village of Sackets Harbor each week to deliver newspapers and letters. All that walking kept Seth skinny as a fence post, and his appetite was famous. "Grandmother's making ginger cakes," Caroline said with a smile.

"I love your grandmother's ginger cakes!" Seth said. Then his grin faded. "Have you had any news about your father and Oliver?"

Caroline kicked a rock. "No," she said. "My birthday's in three weeks, and I *so* hope that Papa will be home by then. But we've had no news from him or Oliver. And we haven't heard from Oliver's parents in weeks, either." Oliver's family—Aunt Martha, Uncle Aaron, and their daughter, Lydia— lived just across the border in Upper Canada. Oliver had been staying with Caroline's family before the war started so that he could learn the shipping trade. He and Lydia had been sailing with Caroline and Papa last June when a British officer and his sailors had seized Oliver's new sloop, *White Gull*. The British had released only Caroline and Lydia.

"I haven't crossed to Canada in a while," Seth said. "Since the war began, most of my customers there have moved away."

Caroline stared over the garden fence. Soldiers had cut many trees as they built blockhouses and log walls to protect the village. Beyond the stumps, the forest was a flaming glory of cardinal red and egg-yolk yellow. She was too worried to enjoy the scene, though. "I wish I could just sail across the lake and find out what's happening!" she exclaimed. The thought of

blockhouse

4

traveling to Upper Canada—maybe even to Kingston, where the British troops were headquartered—made her feel like custard, all quivery. But if she might learn something about Papa and Oliver, or perhaps even see them, she'd make the trip.

"You're running out of time then," Seth said. "It's getting cold for lake travel." He picked up the shovel, pushed it into the hole she'd started, and gave one good heave. The entire plant and all the potatoes clinging to its roots flipped free from the soil.

Caroline stooped and began gathering the potatoes into a basket. "Mama wants to go, too," she told him. "But since she's managing the shipyard now, she's worried about leaving the business."

"This war is a devil of a thing," Seth said grimly. "We won independence from the British thirty years ago. Shouldn't have to fight 'em again."

"Grandmother says it's a waste of time to talk about what can't be changed," Caroline told him. "She says, 'Find something you *can* do to help the situation.'" Caroline sighed. "That isn't always easy to do."

5

The war had brought many changes to Caroline's family and neighbors. In just a few months, their tiny village had become a bustling port. Abbott's Shipyard was building a small gunboat to carry  troops and cannons. Shipwrights at the new navy shipyard nearby were working on a huge warship to fight the British on Lake Ontario. More sailors and carpenters arrived in town every day.

And people keep arriving, Caroline thought. As she picked up the heavy basket, she noticed another newcomer trudging up the lane. Caroline started to turn toward the root cellar, but something made her pause. She squinted at the young man approaching... and then she squealed with joy.

"Oliver! It's *Oliver!*" she cried. Surely Papa would be with him! She dropped the potatoes, lifted her skirt, and raced to meet her cousin. She wrapped him in a hug. His wool coat smelled of sweat and smoke. She didn't know whether to laugh or cry with happiness.

"Oh, Oliver—it's so good to see you!" she said finally, stepping back to drink in the sight of him.

Caroline noticed another newcomer trudging up the lane. She started toward the root cellar, but something made her pause.

Instead of looking happy, though, Oliver looked serious.

Then Caroline realized that the lane behind her cousin was empty. "But—where's Papa?"

Oliver crouched down and took her hands. His face was thin and stubbly with a beard. His eyes were full of shadows. "Your papa isn't with me," he said. "I'm so sorry, Caroline. Two weeks ago the British put me on a boat, sailed me to the American side of the lake, and dropped me off on shore. I was miles from nowhere, and I've been making my way to Sackets Harbor ever since. But they didn't release your father."

Caroline stared at her cousin. She had always imagined Oliver and Papa being set free *together*. But here was Oliver, weary, skinny ... and alone.

"Why wasn't Papa released?" Caroline asked as Grandmother and Seth joined them.

"Someone told the British that he is a master shipbuilder," Oliver said. "The British asked him to work for them. He refused."

"I'd think so!" Seth muttered.

Oliver sighed. "But now they're holding him so that he can't come home and build ships for the American navy."

Caroline's shoulders slumped. Did that mean the British would keep Papa prisoner for the rest of the war? The war might last for years!

Oliver rose to his feet, wobbled a bit, and took a step to steady himself. Grandmother put one hand on his cheek, as if to be sure he was truly there. Her expression was hard, but her voice was gentle. "Welcome home, Oliver. Come along to the house. You need a good meal, a hot bath, and a soft bed."

Oliver looked back at Caroline. He seemed to be waiting for something.

"Welcome home," Caroline echoed. "We're very glad you're here." And it was true—she was so glad to see her cousin again! But her heart still felt heavy as an anchor.

By late afternoon, the Abbotts' kitchen was fragrant with fresh biscuits, baked beans, and potatoes fried with chopped onions. Caroline collected pewter plates and set them on the sturdy table. Ever since Papa had been taken prisoner, she and Mama and Grandmother had eaten every meal in the kitchen. It was comforting to eat near the hearth, with her cat, Inkpot, purring on the braided rug.

She poured mugs of cider for Oliver and Seth. A bath, a nap, and clean clothes had clearly done Oliver good.

"I'm feeling better already," he said. "And I've made a decision. I intend to join the navy."

"But—you just got home!" Caroline protested.

Grandmother's eyes filled with sadness, but she nodded. "I'm proud of you, Oliver."

Caroline looked at her cousin. *He needs our help now,* she thought. "I'm proud of you, too," she whispered.

"Thank you," Oliver said. "It feels so good to be free and to make my own decisions!" Then he sighed. "I'm just sorry the British didn't release Uncle John with me."

Mama drew in a long breath and blew it out again. "That isn't your fault," she told Oliver firmly. "Tonight we will celebrate *your* safe return."

Oliver took a long drink of cider and wiped his mouth with his hand. "There's something else you need to know."

Caroline clenched her hands together in her lap. *Is there more bad news?* she wondered.

"The British have more prisoners than they can handle in Kingston," Oliver said. He glanced at Caroline and then away. "They're planning to send most of them east."

"East!" Caroline cried. "Where?"

Oliver's jaw tightened. "Halifax."

Halifax? Caroline didn't know exactly where Halifax was, but she knew it was far away—all the way to the Atlantic coast.

Trying to ease the sudden pounding of her heart, Caroline got up and reached for her sewing, which she had set on a bench by the fire. Concentrating on her embroidery stitches, she busied her hands and listened to the talk.

"Winter is coming . . . and now this," Mama said grimly. "I can't wait any longer to take action."

Caroline looked up. "We're going to Canada?" she asked hopefully. Perhaps she would see Papa soon after all!

Mama corrected her. "*I* am going to Canada."

Caroline wanted to protest. She longed to see Papa, too! But in her mind, she heard his voice: *I need you to stay steady, Caroline. Obey your mama.* Quickly she looked back down at her work, biting her lip and forcing herself to make perfectly neat, even stitches.

"I will not let the British take my husband to some distant prison without trying to see him," Mama was saying. "Perhaps I can even convince the British officers to release him."

Caroline felt her spirits rise just a little. When the British had tried to capture Sackets Harbor, Mama had stood with Papa's pistol in her hand, ready to defend the shipyard. If anyone could convince the British to release Papa, it was Mama.

"I should be able to sail to Upper Canada in a day," Mama said. "Oliver, I'll let your parents know you are safe and well. I can spend the night at their farm before going on to Kingston."

"Can you handle the skiff by yourself?" Oliver asked. He sounded worried.

Caroline thought about how windy it could be on Lake Ontario. Mama was an experienced sailor, but it would take a lot of strength to sail all the way to Upper Canada. Papa mostly used the little skiff, named *Sparrow*, for fishing in sheltered waters near Sackets Harbor. Kingston, though, was thirty miles away! And storms could blow in quickly on the lake. Oliver was right to worry.

"I'll watch the weather and stay close to shore," Mama promised. "I can always stop to rest or take shelter at the Baxter place."

"No!" Seth said sharply. Then he lowered his voice. "The Baxters are loyal to Great Britain. It wouldn't be safe to stop there."

Caroline felt a sinking sensation in her chest. The Baxters were old family friends who had started a farm on an island just across the border. The Abbotts had often stopped there on visits to Upper Canada. *It's terrible to think that Mama wouldn't be safe with the Baxters,* Caroline thought. She stitched faster, pushing back her fear as she pushed the needle through the cloth.

"This could be a dangerous trip for more reasons than one," Oliver reminded Mama. "I'll go with you. I can help with the skiff, and I'm eager to see my family before I enlist."

Grandmother banged her mug on the table, making everyone jump. "Don't be foolish," she told Oliver. "The British arrested you on an American ship once. If anyone were to spot you in Upper

Canada again, you'd be off to Halifax, too."

"I'm willing to take that risk," Oliver insisted. "I can't just sit here while Uncle John is still being held. The British will never let him come home to build ships for the American navy." He lowered his voice, as if worried that a British soldier might be listening. "Uncle John needs to escape."

"You think Papa might be able to *escape*?" Caroline asked. Sometimes her heart felt like a skiff caught in a windy squall, blown back and forth between hope and despair.

"It wouldn't be easy," Oliver said quickly. "But I've heard about several prisoners who escaped from boats headed for Halifax. A prisoner can quickly slip away and hide in the woods along the Saint Lawrence River." Oliver raked his fingers through his hair. "If I go back, perhaps I could somehow help Uncle John—"

"And who will help *you* escape when you're captured for a second time?" Grandmother demanded. "Not one more word from you about traveling to Kingston."

Oliver looked as if he wanted to argue. Then he reluctantly nodded.

"Mama," Caroline said, "if you *are* allowed to see Papa, perhaps you can whisper to him! Tell him that if the British send him east, that will be his best chance to escape!"

Seth looked at Mama. "The skiff will be easier to handle with a second person along. I'd be glad to escort you, Mrs. Abbott," he offered.

"I can't let you take that risk," Mama said. "My husband is a prisoner. If the British see you with me, they might decide you're in Upper Canada to cause trouble."

"How about taking one of the shipyard workers?" Caroline suggested.

Mama shook her head. "Every man is needed at the yard if the gunboat is to be built on time. Besides, British soldiers will be less suspicious of a woman traveler."

Caroline glanced around the table. Seth and Oliver looked worried. Mama looked determined. And Grandmother... Grandmother was looking intently at *her*, and there seemed to be a message in her eyes.

Suddenly Caroline understood. *Why, Grandmother thinks I should go.* Caroline caught her breath, her needle poised in midstitch. She wasn't as strong as Oliver or Seth, but she could help handle the skiff. Papa had taught her well. Caroline knew the trip would be much safer with two people.

She pulled her thread through the linen and took a deep breath. "You shouldn't travel alone, Mama," she said. "Please let me come with you."

Mama hesitated. "Very well, Caroline," she said finally. "You may come."

Chapter
Two

The Hathaways

Later that evening, after Seth had left, Caroline, Mama, and Grandmother made plans for the journey.

"If the weather is fair, we'll leave in the morning," Mama said.

Caroline smiled, but her stomach did a nervous flip-flop. She and Mama were going to see Papa! Still, the idea of going to Kingston made her anxious.

Suddenly a look of doubt crossed Mama's face. She looked from Caroline to Grandmother. "Perhaps I spoke in haste when I agreed to let Caroline come."

Caroline stared at Mama. "But—"

"I hope you're not thinking to leave her home on my account," Grandmother said sharply.

A log popped and snapped on the fire. Caroline chewed her lip, troubled with fresh worries. Grandmother was a brave woman, but she moved slowly these days. With Oliver joining the navy, could she handle all of the harvesttime chores alone?

A knock on the front door startled everyone. "I'll answer it," Caroline said, tucking her embroidery into her apron pocket.

When Caroline opened the door, she was surprised to see three strangers: a woman, a girl who looked slightly older than Caroline, and a little girl. An American soldier stood behind them.

Caroline could see weariness in the slope of the woman's shoulders, in the older girl's downcast gaze, in the forlorn way the child leaned against her sister. A few snowflakes dotted their cloaks and the woman's travel bag.

"Is this the Abbott house?" the woman asked.

"Yes," Caroline said. "Please come in."

Mama's heels clicked on the hall floor behind her. "Good evening," she said. "I'm Mrs. Abbott. This is my daughter, Caroline."

The woman pushed back the hood of her cloak. She had brown hair and a thin face and wore narrow spectacles. "I'm Mrs. Hathaway," she said. "These are *my* daughters. The little one is Amelia, and this is Rhonda."

Rhonda was a few inches taller than Caroline, and she wore her auburn hair fixed in a fancy style. She smiled shyly as she pulled off her wool mittens.

Mrs. Hathaway adjusted her spectacles. "My husband is an army officer. We've traveled from Albany with his regiment, and I've spent the last hour looking for lodging. Most people are already full up with boarders."

No wonder the girls look tired, Caroline thought.

"Even a small space would be welcome," Mrs. Hathaway added. "We sometimes slept in a tent on our journey. We're quite used to making do."

Caroline and Mama exchanged a glance, and Caroline could tell that they were both thinking the same thing. "We have plenty of room," Caroline said.

Mrs. Hathaway smiled with relief. "You may report back to my husband," she told the soldier who had escorted her and the girls. "We've found a place to stay."

Oliver offered to sleep in the kitchen, leaving the spare bedroom for the Hathaways. Mrs. Hathaway and Amelia, who was four, would sleep in the bed. Mama helped Rhonda make a pallet on the floor with coverlets and blankets. "We'll make a cornhusk mattress for you, too," Mama assured Rhonda.

"We're grateful for your hospitality," Mrs. Hathaway declared. "In addition to paying for room and board, I'll be glad to help with chores."

Mama looked thoughtful. "Mrs. Hathaway, Caroline and I will be traveling for a few days. We hope to leave tomorrow."

"Grandmother is used to doing all the cooking," Caroline added. "Still, Mama and I are worried about leaving her alone."

"Worry no longer," Mrs. Hathaway said briskly. "Now, it's Amelia's bedtime."

"Come downstairs when you get her settled, and we'll have hot tea waiting," Mama promised. "Caroline, why don't you and Rhonda get acquainted?"

Caroline's eyes widened as Rhonda removed her cloak and bonnet. Her flowing, high-waisted green gown was trimmed with lace the color of eggshells.

She looked elegant! Caroline glanced from Mama's sturdy work dress to her own skirt, which was splattered with mud from the garden. Had Rhonda worn that fine dress for long days of rough travel?

"Caroline?" Mama prompted.

Caroline's cheeks grew hot. "I'll show you my bedchamber, Rhonda," she said.

Caroline led Rhonda to her room. It was small and narrow, but Caroline loved having a space of her own. Best of all, it faced north, so Caroline could sit by her window and see the water.

Rhonda's gaze settled on a mahogany worktable. "That's pretty."

"Papa gave it to me because I love to sew," Caroline explained. "I'm going to turn ten in three weeks, and I'm making a new dress for my birthday." She opened the worktable and pulled out several pieces of lovely blue cloth.

"I like the color," Rhonda said.

"It reminds me of Lake Ontario on a sunny day," Caroline told her. "If we could still shop in Kingston, I'd buy some lace trim."

"My mother is teaching me to
make lace with thread and a little
shuttle," Rhonda said.

Rhonda knew how to *make* lace?
"I've never seen anyone do that,"
Caroline admitted. "But I do like to embroider." She
proudly pulled her current project from her apron
pocket. "My papa loves Lake Ontario, and I've been
stitching a map of the lakeshore for him."

"But . . . whatever will he do with it?" Rhonda
asked.

Something about the way Rhonda asked the
question made Caroline wish she'd just put the
embroidery away in the worktable instead of showing
it off. "One of the carpenters at my family's shipyard
has promised to frame my embroidery as a fire
screen," she told Rhonda. Caroline loved to imagine

Papa relaxing by the hearth in the
evenings, shielded from the fire's
heat by the screen.

Rhonda's gaze wandered from
the embroidery. "What's that?" she
asked, pointing at a short length of
knotted rope inside the worktable.

Caroline stroked the knots with one finger. "The British are holding my papa prisoner in Kingston because he's a shipbuilder. He was teaching me how to tie different knots. We were working on this together while we were out sailing the day he was captured."

"Oh, I see." Rhonda's mouth closed in a very tight line. She turned away as if she weren't interested.

Our life must seem boring to someone who comes from a big city like Albany and who knows how to make lace, Caroline thought. She tucked her treasures back into the worktable and closed the lid. "Grandmother likely has the tea ready," she said. "Let's go down to the kitchen."

❖

The next morning, Mama woke Caroline before dawn. "The sky is cloudy, but there's no sign of storms," Mama said. "We'll sail today. Grandmother is cooking breakfast."

Caroline quickly dressed and hurried downstairs. Soon she would be in Upper Canada, where Papa was! Upper Canada, where enemy soldiers and sailors were headquartered. By the time Caroline sat down to crisp bacon, biscuits warm from the oven, and a bowl of steaming oatmeal, her stomach seemed to be tying itself into knots that any sailor would envy.

The Hathaways filed into the kitchen as Caroline was struggling to finish her meal. "Please, sit down," Caroline said. "I'll fetch more bowls."

She was reaching for the ladle in the oatmeal pot when an odd knock sounded on the front door. *Knock...knock-knock. Knock...knock-knock.*

"Father!" Amelia squealed. She raced from the kitchen. Rhonda's face lit up with joy as she hurried after her sister.

"It's his special knock," Mrs. Hathaway explained. "Please, come—he'll want to meet you."

Grandmother started to rise, but then winced in pain and sank back onto her chair. "The oatmeal will scorch if I don't keep an eye on it," she said. "You two go."

Caroline and Mama found a tall man standing in the hall. He held Amelia on one hip and had his other arm around Rhonda.

Caroline's feet decided to stop walking.

Mama paused, bending close. "Caroline? Are you well?"

"Yes, fine," she whispered. She didn't want to admit to Mama that the sight of Rhonda and Amelia greeting their father had given her a stab of envy.

After introductions were made, Lieutenant Hathaway bowed to Mama and Caroline. "Thank you for sheltering my family," he said. "With your permission, I will visit often. But now I must return to my duties."

"You may come any time," Mama assured him. "Caroline, why don't we go pack and let the Hathaways say their good-byes."

Caroline was glad to leave the Hathaways behind. Once upstairs, she set out two heavy wool shawls, her flannel petticoat, and warm gloves. Mama brought her a canvas sack that was coated with wax to keep out water.

"May I take my embroidery?" Caroline asked. "When I'm worried, it helps me to stitch."

"That's a fine idea," Mama said. "I think I shall take my knitting, for much the same reason."

Mrs. Hathaway and Rhonda decided to see the Abbotts off. "We need to get familiar with Sackets Harbor," Mrs. Hathaway said. She and Mama walked ahead of the two girls.

Caroline was so excited and nervous about the trip that she wanted to run straight to the harbor. Still, she tried to make Rhonda feel comfortable. "You can't get lost in the village," Caroline assured her as they turned right onto the main street. "This road leads to the marketplace and the harbor." She pointed ahead.

"It *would* be hard to get lost in such a tiny village," Rhonda remarked.

Caroline felt her cheeks grow hot. She was getting tired of Rhonda Hathaway acting superior! Rhonda might wear fancy clothes, and know how to make lace, and have a papa she could see every single day. But Caroline refused to let Rhonda make her feel ashamed of her home.

Instead, Caroline lifted her chin the way her cousin Lydia did when she wanted to look like a fine lady. "I suppose Sackets Harbor *is* small compared to Albany," Caroline said, her tone chilly as an October lake. "But it's growing fast."

In truth, Caroline hardly recognized her village. Since the war began, the streets had become so crowded! She saw noisy sailors wearing dirty canvas trousers and bright shirts. Stiff-backed marines in blue coats with white crossbelts over their chests marched crisply down the road. And local farmers and clerks who'd joined the militia strode by wearing whatever they pleased.

The frosty morning was filled with commotion. Workmen pounded hammers and manned big saws. Officers bellowed orders. Local farmwives who had set up shop in the marketplace called to passersby. Horses clopped past. Occasionally, Caroline heard the shuddering boom of artillery or the sharp pop of musketry as soldiers practiced.

"Being around soldiers must seem strange to you," Rhonda said coolly. "I'm accustomed to it. This isn't the first time we've traveled with my father's regiment. We like being close to him."

Caroline felt another stab of jealousy. She pointed ahead. "There's *my* papa's shipyard," she said proudly. "He and his men are the best shipbuilders in New York."

Rhonda flushed pink. "Well, *my* father—"

"Come along, girls," Mama called, turning to beckon them forward. Caroline thought that Mama looked nervous and excited, too.

Mr. Tate hurried to meet them. "Good morning," he said, eyeing the bags Caroline and Mama carried. "Today's the day, eh?"

He already understands where we're going, Caroline thought. She smiled gratefully at Mr. Tate. She knew that Mama dared leave the shipyard only because she trusted him to handle things.

Mama introduced the Hathaways and then said, "Mr. Tate, I need to speak with you in the office about what must be done here in the next few days."

"I'll be right along, ma'am," Mr. Tate said. He was a big man, and weathered from his years as a sailor. His straw hat had been caked with tar to shed rain. His corduroy jacket was well worn. Mr. Tate didn't care about fancy clothes, but he knew more about shaping wood into ships than just about anyone.

"I wish you good luck on your journey, Miss Caroline," Mr. Tate said.

"Thank you," Caroline said. Then she leaned close and whispered, "I'm so excited I might burst!

28

I don't know if I should feel hopeful or worried."

"If anyone can convince the British to release your father, it's Mrs. Abbott," he told Caroline. "So all you need to worry about is getting home in time for your birthday." His eyes twinkled. "I hear there's a special dinner planned. Mrs. Abbott was kind enough to invite me."

"I'm trying to decide whether to ask Grandmother for an apple pie or a burnt-sugar cake," Caroline told him.

Mr. Tate grinned. "Fine eating either way. And I have a special gift in mind for my favorite young lady."

"Thank you, Mr. Tate." Caroline gave him a warm smile.

Mr. Tate hurried to the office. Mrs. Hathaway left the girls and wandered away to look over the yard. Caroline turned her attention to the gunboat the men were building. It was a heavy ship with a flat bottom, perfect for traveling through the shallow waters along Lake Ontario's shore and in the Saint Lawrence River nearby.

Caroline had many different feelings when she visited the shipyard these days. She missed Papa's

quiet presence terribly, but she was also proud of
Mama and the workers. "That gunboat will carry
troops and equipment, and maybe go into battle, too,"
she explained to Rhonda. "Mr. Tate and the workers
have done a wonderful job."

"I heard Mr. Tate say he's coming to your
birthday dinner," Rhonda murmured. "He must
know your family very well."

Caroline turned around. "Mr. Tate started
working for Papa before I was born. He looks out
for Mama and me."

"How nice that you have someone to take your
father's place," Rhonda said.

For a moment, Caroline could hardly breathe.
"Why—no, it's not like that at all!" she stammered.
As if someone, *anyone*, could take Papa's place at the
shipyard or in her heart! It was a terrible thing to
suggest.

Rhonda tugged one of her mittens up over her
wrist. "All I meant was that it must be nice to have
someone like—"

"*Nothing* is nice right now!" Caroline cried. "You
don't know what it's like to have your father gone."

"I do know," Rhonda retorted. "My father's

been in the army my whole life. If we didn't follow him every time he was posted somewhere new, I'd probably never see him!"

"It's *not* the same," Caroline insisted. Suddenly all of her worry and envy and nervousness turned into anger. "I wish you *hadn't* followed your papa this time. I wish you'd stayed in Albany!"

Rhonda's eyes narrowed. Then she turned her back on Caroline and walked away.

I shouldn't have spoken so, Caroline thought. Her words had been truthful, but also unkind.

Before she could decide what to do, Mama stepped from the office. "Caroline?" she called. "Let's get started."

As Mama and Caroline settled into the skiff, Caroline tried to put the argument with Rhonda out of her mind. They were off to find Papa. Nothing was more important than that.

CHAPTER
THREE

—

ON ENEMY GROUND

Mama began to row the skiff through the harbor. Several honking geese flew past. Caroline heard sailors on a nearby schooner bellowing "Heave, heave, heave!" as they raised a sail. Perhaps they would head out to search for British ships. *And we're heading out on a dangerous trip, too,* Caroline thought.

Once they reached the open lake Mama paused, shrugging her shoulders to ease her muscles. "The wind is perfect today," she said.

Caroline lifted her face and tried to consider the wind against her cheeks as Papa had taught her. "The breeze seems strong, but not *too* strong," she agreed. "Shall we set the sail?"

As Caroline raised the sail, her spirits lifted, too. She hadn't traveled on Lake Ontario in all the months since the British had captured Papa. In spite of her worries, being back on the water made her happy. She closed her eyes for a moment, feeling the skiff bob on the choppy water. *Papa will come home*, Caroline told herself. She'd prove herself steady enough to make a good captain. And one day Papa would build a sloop just for her.

The skiff rose on a little wave and then dropped again. Caroline's eyes flew open as an icy spray of water hit her face.

"Try not to get splashed," Mama warned. Her cheeks were already bright red from cold.

Caroline wiped her cheek with one hand. The wind that filled their sail also knifed through her cloak. This was a dangerous time of year to travel in such a small boat. If a storm blew up and swamped the little skiff, she and Mama might freeze before reaching shore or getting rescued.

"I'll stay dry," Caroline promised. "Knowing that Papa built this skiff makes me feel safe. It's almost as if he's here, taking care of us. And maybe Papa will soon be sailing it himself!"

As Caroline raised the sail, her spirits lifted, too. She hadn't traveled on Lake Ontario in all the months since the British had captured Papa.

Mama smiled. "That's a lovely thought."

As they settled in for the long journey, Caroline found her mind bouncing between thoughts of Papa and thoughts of the quarrel she'd had with Rhonda that morning. *You can mend things with Rhonda when you get home,* Caroline told herself. Still, Rhonda's comments echoed in her mind.

"Mama," Caroline said finally, "Mr. Tate said you'd invited him to my birthday dinner."

"I did," Mama said. "I want the evening to be special."

Caroline heard Rhonda's voice again: *How nice that you have someone to take your father's place.* "All I want is Papa home for my birthday," Caroline said.

Mama's face softened. "We both want that, and I pray that he will be. But even if he isn't, we'll have a real party. Now that the Hathaways have come, there will be lots of people to celebrate your birthday."

Caroline looked out over the restless water. "I think... that is, I'd rather have just family at my birthday dinner."

"I see," Mama said slowly. "Don't you like Rhonda? I thought it would be nice for you to have another girl in the house."

35

"I don't want another girl in the house," Caroline grumbled. She felt tears threaten and blinked hard to hold them back. "And Mr. Tate can never take Papa's place!"

Mama looked startled. "Of *course* not! But today, let's think just about getting Papa home, shall we?"

Caroline's cheeks grew hot with embarrassment. She was determined to be helpful on this trip. Fretting about her quarrel with Rhonda wouldn't help anything.

"Yes," she agreed firmly. "Let's think just about getting Papa home."

The trip took all day. Mama sailed close to shore as they traveled, threading their way around islands. She landed the skiff several times on deserted beaches so that she and Caroline could stretch their legs, rub their arms for warmth, and snack on bread and apples.

Caroline felt that knotted feeling in her stomach again as they reached the north shore of the Saint Lawrence River. That mighty river marked the border between New York and Upper Canada. *We're in enemy territory now,* she thought. She didn't see any British ships, but she knew they must be patrolling nearby.

As Caroline watched the wooded shoreline of Upper Canada glide by, she imagined Papa slipping away from his guards and hiding in the forest. Sometimes she and Mama sailed past Indian camps or little clearings where settlers had built log homes. The shelters and cabins looked no different from those Caroline knew in New York. It seemed so strange to think that the people who lived in them were likely loyal to the British!

Finally Mama said, "We're getting close to Uncle Aaron and Aunt Martha's farm. You've done well today, Caroline."

Mama's praise made Caroline feel good, and she was glad she hadn't complained about the cold or her growing hunger. Still, by the time the cabin came into view a few miles east of Kingston, Caroline felt hollow and frozen to the bone. Her arms ached from helping with the oars. She used her last bit of strength to help Mama pull the skiff up on the shore.

Lydia and Oliver's parents had moved their

family to Upper Canada a few years before the war began, when the border between the two countries hardly seemed to matter at all. Caroline knew they'd worked hard to build their small cabin and clear a few acres to farm.

Twilight was falling as Caroline and Mama hurried into the yard. "It seems very quiet," Mama murmured.

Caroline looked around. The clearing seemed deserted. *Oh no*, she thought with dismay. *What will we do if no one is home?*

Mama strode to the front door and knocked. A curtain over the front window twitched, as if someone was peeping out.

Mama knocked again. "Aaron?" she called. "It's your sister!"

The door finally opened, and Uncle Aaron appeared. Caroline had never been so glad to see her uncle!

"Come inside, quickly," he said. His tone was hushed, and his gaze darted nervously about the empty farmyard.

Caroline followed him and Mama into the cabin.

Lydia hurried forward and crushed Caroline into
a hug.

"We've got news," Mama said. "Oliver is free!
He arrived at our house yesterday."

Aunt Martha caught her breath, and her eyes
filled with tears. Uncle Aaron whispered, "God be
praised." Lydia squeezed Caroline's hand.

Then Uncle Aaron cleared his throat. "It's
wonderful to see you both, and we want to hear
more. But first—did you sail over?"

"Our skiff is down on the beach," Caroline said.

"We'll have to hide it," Uncle Aaron said.
"Martha, Lydia, come help with the boat. Caroline,
you stay here and warm up."

Lydia followed her parents and Mama outside.
Alone in the cabin, Caroline shivered with fear
as much as cold. Why was Uncle Aaron acting so
strange? And why was he so worried about the
skiff?

She sank onto a stool by the big hearth and stared
at the crackling flames. A kettle of stew bubbled
over the fire. The room smelled of cider vinegar,
hickory smoke, venison, and molasses pie. Caroline
breathed in the comforting harvesttime scents.

When her fingers were warm enough, she tugged off her gloves, reached into her travel bag, and pulled out her embroidery. *I'm glad I brought this*, she thought, even though she had to lean toward the fire to see well enough to stitch. She smoothed the embroidery over her lap and studied it, thinking of the colors Lake Ontario showed on sunny days. She decided to add streaks of green to the blue water she'd already created with silk thread. The familiar challenge of blending colors occupied her thoughts and calmed her hands.

By the time the others returned, Caroline's shivering had stopped. "We're glad you're here," Aunt Martha said. She kissed Caroline's cheek. "We'll dish up some stew. You'll feel better after a hot meal."

Caroline tucked her embroidery away. Uncle Aaron sat down on the far side of the hearth and gestured Mama into another chair. "I'm sorry if I didn't seem welcoming," he said to Caroline. "These are dangerous times. We've learned to be cautious when we hear voices outside. It might be friends coming, or it might be Loyalists—people who support the British."

Caroline's fingers trembled as she accepted a bowl from Lydia. The stew was thick with tender chunks of venison, potatoes, and carrots. After one bite, Caroline felt a little better.

Uncle Aaron took his clay pipe from its holder near the hearth, filled the bowl with tobacco, and used a long curled wood shaving to light it. "Since the war began, things have become difficult for newcomers like us," he explained. "People who settled here thirty years ago suspect that we are still Americans at heart and not truly loyal to King George. They think we moved north only to gain farmland."

"And they are right," Aunt Martha murmured. She ladled stew into another wooden bowl.

"I wanted to stay out of this war altogether," Uncle Aaron said. "But by law I must serve in the British militia. I could be called to duty any moment."

"Oh no," Caroline whispered. Uncle Aaron might end up fighting his former friends and neighbors! She glanced at Lydia and saw misery in her cousin's face.

Uncle Aaron sighed. "I've examined my heart. I cannot stay here and fight for the king. So Martha

41

and I have decided to move back to New York. We've been building a boat—secretly, in the woods. If our luck holds, we'll finish the boat in time to cross the Saint Lawrence River before it ices over. But if our Loyalist neighbors realize what we're doing, we could be arrested as traitors."

Caroline gasped. Traitors could be imprisoned— or hanged. She put her bowl down, no longer hungry.

"We believe some of our neighbors are spying on us already," Lydia added. She crossed her arms over her chest, clutching her shoulders as if she were cold.

Now Caroline understood why Uncle Aaron had wanted to hide the skiff. If the Loyalists saw it, they might think he was planning to use it to escape back to New York. "Please be careful," she begged.

"We will," Uncle Aaron promised. But even in the flickering firelight, worry showed on his face. "Now, please tell us about Oliver—is he well?"

Mama and Caroline told the story of Oliver's release. "He's worn down, but he'll be fine," Mama finished.

"He brought bad news, though," Caroline said. "He told us that the British are planning to send prisoners to Halifax. Oliver thinks that if Papa ends up on a ship to Halifax, he should try to escape."

"That's why we're here," Mama said. "I'm going to argue for my husband's release. If I fail, I'll try to let him know what Oliver advises."

Uncle Aaron got to his feet and began to pace the room. "But if John does escape, what then? The weather is already harsh, and it will only get colder. How would he get back to New York?"

"Papa could do it!" Caroline insisted. Her aunt glanced nervously toward the door, and Caroline lowered her voice. "He knows this end of the lake as well as anybody—"

"That won't keep him safe," Uncle Aaron broke in. "Yes, he knows the marshes and the currents. And at one time, he knew everyone who lived along these shores. But that's no longer enough."

Aunt Martha explained, "Your father has no way of knowing which families he can trust, or where the British gunboats patrol. If the British were to capture him a second time, he would be treated much more harshly."

"Then we must get him the information he needs," Mama said briskly. "Perhaps I can tuck a note between the pages of the Bible I brought, or hide it away in some food. Surely the British won't stop a worried wife from bringing her husband a Bible and a cake!"

"If you're allowed to visit him at all," Uncle Aaron said grimly, "whatever you carry will be searched. And if you're caught with such a note, you'll be arrested."

Lydia slipped her hand into Caroline's. "I wish we were *all* safe in Sackets Harbor," she whispered.

Caroline wished the skiff were big enough to carry everyone back to New York. She wished she could cuddle Inkpot's rumbling warmth against her cheek. She wished she were as brave as her grandmother.

Oh, Grandmother, she thought, *everything is even worse than we feared.*

And there in the little cabin in enemy territory, miles from home and safety, Caroline fancied she could hear Grandmother's answer: *It is, eh? Well, what are you going to do about it? Come now, girl. You're not giving up, are you?*

I don't want to give up, Caroline protested silently. But how could *she* help get Papa the information he needed?

This time, Grandmother didn't answer.

Caroline reached for her embroidery and ran a finger over the map she'd stitched so carefully. *We're right here*, she thought, touching the spot where Lydia's cabin stood. Then she ran her finger over the smooth stitches that formed the nearby shoreline. *If Papa is able to escape, he'll need to follow this route to safety . . .*

"Oh!" she said suddenly. "I have an idea!"

45

PAPA

After an early breakfast the next morning, Mama and Caroline sailed on to Kingston. Caroline was excited and nervous and tired. She had sat up late the night before, working carefully on her embroidered map. Uncle Aaron and Aunt Martha had identified the location of every old friend who could no longer be trusted, as well as waterways patrolled most often by British gunboats. Caroline had carefully stitched a warning X at each trouble spot.

Now her heart seemed to bang against her ribs as they approached Point Frederick, where Papa was being held. She hadn't been so close to Papa in months. She had to clench her teeth to keep from yelling, *Mama and I are here, Papa! We've come to help you escape!*

As she and Mama pulled the skiff up on the beach, a young soldier trotted toward them. He wore white trousers and a scarlet coat with a white crossbelt. His musket held a long bayonet. His black-and-gold hat was so tall that he looked especially threatening.

"Mama," Caroline whispered. Her knees felt wobbly.

Mama squeezed Caroline's shoulder. "Have courage, Caroline. If we are not able to win Papa's release, his best chance of escape depends on you and your map."

The soldier reached them. "Madam," he began, "this is a military area."

"I understand that, sir," Mama said. "But my husband is being held here unjustly. I came to see whoever is in charge."

"That's Major Humphries," he said stiffly. "Follow me."

The soldier led them into the fort area. *In truth,* Caroline thought, *there is not much here!* She saw only a single two-story blockhouse. Hammers banged as soldiers labored to build a rough wall around the grounds. A civilian man was yelling at an ox pulling a wagon piled with lumber.

She stumbled over a rut left by wagon wheels, but she couldn't tear her gaze from the buildings. Papa was *here*! Was he in that building? Or that other one, over there? Was he watching them through one of the windows? She trembled with the longing to run and search, calling for him.

Mama took Caroline's hand and gave her a warning look: *I know it's difficult to stay calm. But we must not do anything to anger the soldiers.*

The soldier took them to one of the wooden buildings and explained his errand to another sentry. Finally Mama and Caroline were led into a large room that was surprisingly well furnished. A tall chest of drawers gleamed with polish. A mirror hung on one wall, and silver candlesticks and crystal goblets sparkled on a side table.

A stern, gray-haired man with red cheeks sat at a table. He was eating beans and bacon from a china plate. A cup of tea steamed beside it. Several papers were fanned on the

Caroline couldn't tear her gaze from the buildings. Was Papa in that building? Or that one, over there?

table in front of the man's breakfast.

He wiped his mouth on a linen handkerchief and rose to meet Mama and Caroline. "I'm Major Humphries. You're looking for one of the prisoners, I'm told." He waved his hand toward two chairs. "Please, sit."

Mama introduced them. Caroline perched on the edge of her chair. It seemed impossible that they were truly here, inside a British fort, talking to a British officer!

"You've been holding my husband, John Abbott, since last June," Mama began. "He was taken from a merchant ship before we knew that war had been declared. His absence makes life very difficult for me and my daughter."

Caroline tried to look frightened and needy. That part wasn't hard.

"So I ask you, sir, to release my husband," Mama finished. "He's done nothing wrong."

The major shook his head. "I'm sorry, madam. We know Mr. Abbott is a shipbuilder. We simply cannot release him."

Mama sat very tall, her hands clenched in her lap. For a moment she pressed her lips together. Finally she said, "Well then, sir, I would like to see my husband."

He shook his head. "Can't be done."

"Sir," Mama said sharply, "surely you will not be so unkind! I have brought a bit of food, a Bible, and a warm shirt. My husband was taken in springtime, and now winter is on its way."

A burst of laughter rang from one of the next rooms. Caroline felt anger rise hot in her chest. How she hated those soldiers and their carefree laughter! She hated Major Humphries and his china plate full of food and his fancy furniture. She hated the British flags hanging on his walls.

Major Humphries rubbed his nose. "This country is full of spies, madam. Just last week a woman selling sweet potatoes tried to smuggle a message to one of the prisoners. No. My answer is no."

Caroline stared at him. She didn't think she could bear to be so close to Papa without being permitted to see him.

"Sir, I *beg* you." Mama's voice trembled. "I have not seen my husband in four months. I—I need to know that he is well."

"I assure you, he is well. And that is the best

I can do for you." Major Humphries beckoned to
the soldier who had brought them. "Jenner, escort
these ladies to their boat. They're going home."

"Please, sir!" Caroline cried desperately.
"I haven't seen my papa in ever so long." One tear
slid down her cheek, and she didn't wipe it away.
"Do you have any daughters?"

Major Humphries studied her. Caroline forced
herself to look back at him. The shrill and rattle of
a fife and drum drifted into the room.

Finally the officer sighed. "I do, child,
I do. They're all grown now, but no less
dear to me for that." He looked at Jenner.
"Take the child to see her father. A *short*
visit, mind! Mrs. Abbott, you may wait
in the hall."

Mama took Caroline's hand. "Give Papa
my love," she said. The look in her eyes gave Caroline
another message: *And give Papa the information he
needs to make a safe escape!*

The knots in Caroline's stomach pulled tighter.
She was about to see Papa! But she had never imagined
visiting him without Mama. *Be brave,* she commanded
herself. It was time to stitch together her courage.

Jenner led Caroline across the yard to the blockhouse, where another guard was on duty. He had a long scar on one cheek. Caroline didn't want to think about how he might have gotten that scar.

"The major said she could see Mr. Abbott," Jenner explained to the blockhouse guard. "We need to search her cloak and her basket."

Caroline's skin felt prickly—so much depended on the next few minutes! She placed her basket on a small table by the door. Then she unfastened her cloak and handed it to the guard.

The guard checked the seams and lining to see if she'd hidden anything between the layers of cloth. Jenner poked through Caroline's basket. He turned the wool shirt inside out. He flipped through the small Bible, holding it upside down to make sure no slips of paper had been tucked between the pages. He inspected the bag of apples and dried cherries.

Then the guard pulled out the ginger cakes that Grandmother had sent along and crumbled them in his fingers. "Sorry," he muttered. "Can't be too careful."

The destruction made Caroline angry, but she only

nodded. *The cakes don't matter,* she told herself. As long as the soldiers let her keep her embroidery, they could take whatever else they wished.

"What's this?" Corporal Jenner was staring into the basket. The only thing left was her embroidered map, folded neatly with the stitches inside.

Caroline's heart thumped so loudly that she was surprised he couldn't hear it. "I—it's just some sewing. I wanted . . . that is, when I'm feeling scared, it helps to keep my hands busy." She hated admitting her fear to these soldiers, but it was the truth.

The guard lifted the cloth, made sure nothing was hidden underneath, and piled everything back into the basket. "All right then."

Caroline blew out her breath. The map was safe!

"Follow me," Jenner commanded. He began clomping up the steps.

Just as Caroline turned to follow him, she heard a low voice, almost a whisper, behind her: "Your father misses you."

Caroline whipped her head around and stared at the guard with the scarred cheek. Had he actually *said* that? His face was expressionless, and he jerked his head toward the stairs.

Caroline hurried after Jenner, up the stairs to a small landing. She found herself facing a closed door. Jenner opened it, calling, "Mr. Abbott? Someone to see—"

"*Papa!*" Caroline had barely even glimpsed him, silhouetted against the window, before she barreled into his arms.

"Caroline?" Papa said hoarsely. "Oh, my own dear Caroline!" He squeezed her so tightly that she could hardly breathe. She squeezed back, breathing in his Papa-scent.

The two of them might have stayed so forever if Jenner hadn't coughed to get their attention. Suddenly Caroline remembered Major Humphries' last order: "A *short* visit, mind!" Reluctantly, she pulled herself from Papa's arms.

The room held a cot with a straw mattress and a small table. The table was littered with scraps of wood. Caroline recognized her father's work in a partially completed model sloop. He'd always enjoyed working with his hands, especially making model ships. Caroline was grateful that the guards had provided him with simple tools and supplies.

"You, sit on the bed," Jenner told Papa. "And you,

miss, sit over here." He pointed Caroline to a chair. "You two have ten minutes to talk."

"Caroline, quickly, give me news," Papa said. "How is everyone at home?"

"We're all well," Caroline said firmly. "Mama is here, but the major wouldn't let her see you. Grandmother has some aches, but she's well too. But... how are *you*?" Papa was much thinner than she remembered. His shirt was dirty, with several neatly mended rips. His eyes were the same, though, and his gentle smile.

"I'm well also," he said. "Missing you all terribly, of course. But the guards have been kind. I'm allowed to stroll about outside sometimes. One guard plays a game of chess or dominoes with me every day."

Caroline was glad for those things, but looking at the model sloop made her heart ache. Papa was a sailor at heart! He needed to be out on open water, not caged in a tiny room.

She glanced at Jenner. He leaned against the wall, watching.

I can feel sad for Papa later, she reminded herself. Right now she had important work to do, and not much time to do it.

She forced down a wave of panic and tried to look calm as she began to unpack the basket. "I brought you a few things, Papa."

"Leave them on the table," Jenner ordered.

Caroline carefully placed the shirt, the fruit, the crumbled cakes, and the Bible beside the wood scraps.

"Thank you," Papa said. He looked very happy with the gifts.

Caroline glanced again at Jenner, who stared back. She felt as if a clock were ticking inside her chest. She pulled her sewing from the basket, her fingers slick with sweat. She had trouble grasping the needle she'd left threaded with green silk.

"Please, Caroline, talk to me of home," Papa said urgently.

While Caroline tried to think of a way to give Papa the information he needed, she rambled nervously from one story to the next. She'd put up six crocks of pickles, but the bean crop had been poor. Grandmother was still helping her learn to bake bread. Inkpot's latest game involved dropping dead mice by her bed.

And all the while, time raced past.

"Just a few more minutes," Jenner warned.

I have to try! Caroline thought desperately. She might never have another chance. *Papa* might never have another chance.

Just then, men started shouting somewhere outside. "What in heaven's name?" Jenner muttered. He stepped to the window.

Now! Caroline thought. She forced herself to go on with her story. "... and Mrs. Shaw set a pan of new soap out to dry in the sun..."

As Caroline spoke, she quickly spread her embroidery against the side of her leg, holding it so that Papa could see the map. It showed the eastern tip of Lake Ontario, which she'd created carefully from silk thread. With one shaking finger, Caroline pointed at the new black X she'd stitched on the island where the Baxter family lived—an X to signal *Don't go here. It's not safe.*

Papa glanced at the map and then back at her. He looked puzzled. Caroline met his gaze fiercely, willing him to understand what she was trying to tell him. "... and the next time Mrs. Shaw looked out her window," she continued, "she saw a raccoon nibbling at that soap."

Caroline pointed at the new black X she'd stitched—
an X *to signal* Don't go here. It's not safe.

Caroline dared a glance at Jenner, who was still watching some commotion in the yard below. Then she moved her finger to another X.

Papa looked completely baffled.

Oh, Papa, please understand! Caroline begged silently. Moving only her finger, she pointed straight at Papa. Then she touched the X and shook her head slightly. *Not—safe!* She mouthed the words silently.

"Blasted oxen are nothing but trouble," Jenner mumbled as he turned away from the window.

Oh no! Caroline thought. She hadn't had a chance to point out every X! Did Papa even understand? She needed more time.

She bent her head and pretended to stitch on one edge of the fabric, leaving the embroidery draped casually over her lap so that Papa could see it. What would happen if Jenner spotted her trick? Would he arrest *her*? Would he punish Papa?

Her voice sounded breathless as she tried to continue her story. "So—so now Seth jokes that we've got the cleanest raccoons in New York."

She darted a glance at Papa. He was studying the map intensely now. "And then—"

"That's all," Jenner said. "Time for you to go."

Caroline's heart felt ready to crack in two.

"Oh, my dear daughter," Papa whispered.

Without asking for permission from Jenner, Caroline ran to her father and gave him another hug. "I'm trying to stay steady," she whispered. "I'm trying to ride the storms through to better weather."

Papa held her close for a moment before gently pulling away. "That's my girl," he said. He swiped at his eyes and then gave her a firm look. "Thank you for coming, Caroline. Thank you for the shirt and the fruit and the Bible." He let his gaze flick to the embroidered map as she folded it back into her basket. "Thank you for *everything.*"

HAPPY BIRTHDAY, CAROLINE

"Almost home," Mama said the next evening as they turned onto their lane in Sackets Harbor. A cold rain had begun to fall. Caroline couldn't remember being so tired. When their house came into view, though, she saw that Grandmother had put a candle in the window. The tiny glow made her feel warm and safe.

"Let's go in the back door," Mama suggested. "Grandmother is likely in the kitchen."

Caroline heard raised voices and laughter as she and Mama walked around the house. *The Hathaways must be in the kitchen with Grandmother,* Caroline thought. She was glad that Grandmother had not been alone while she and Mama were gone. When she remembered saying that she wished Rhonda hadn't followed her father to Sackets Harbor, her face felt hot. She didn't like what Rhonda had said to her about Mr. Tate taking Papa's place. Still, Caroline knew she owed Rhonda an apology.

The kitchen smelled richly of fish and cabbage and spiced cider. Grandmother was sitting by the fire, knitting. And seated at the table were Mrs. Hathaway, the two girls—and their father. Caroline forgot all about her apology.

Lieutenant Hathaway jumped to his feet. "Why, it's Mrs. Abbott and Miss Caroline!"

The room grew noisy with greetings, but Caroline couldn't join in. After having to leave Papa in Upper Canada, seeing Lieutenant Hathaway sitting with *his* family made her hands curl into fists. Papa was the one who should be sitting in this warm kitchen drinking cider!

"I'm happy you're home," Grandmother said, "but sorry to see that you came without John."

Mama shook her head. "The British would not release him."

Mrs. Hathaway took their damp cloaks and hung them up to dry. Grandmother poured cups of hot cider. Amelia carefully passed them around.

Rhonda was the only person who hadn't stood. "I—I'm sorry you weren't able to win your father's freedom," she said to Caroline.

"Oh, my papa will be home soon," Caroline said. Her voice came out louder than she had planned. "*I* showed him the information he needs to escape!"

After a startled silence, Mama said, "Well, we *hope* he will be home soon."

Rhonda's hand was moving beneath the table. Caroline leaned closer to see what she was doing. Why... Rhonda was petting Inkpot, who was curled up on her lap!

That was just too much to bear. Caroline ran from the kitchen, pounded up the stairs, and threw herself onto her bed. She was crying into her pillow when she heard footsteps enter the room a few minutes later. Mama sat on the bed beside her.

"It's not *fair*," Caroline said through tears. "This is our house, and *my* papa should be here. And—and while we were away, Rhonda stole Inkpot!"

Mama stroked Caroline's hair. "I'm sure Rhonda did not set out to steal Inkpot, Caroline."

Caroline sniffled miserably.

"Have you thought about how Inkpot felt to have you gone?" Mama asked. "He was probably lonely without you. And Rhonda is probably lonely, too. She's new here in Sackets Harbor, remember."

"I know," Caroline grumbled.

"You were strong and brave on our trip to Upper Canada," Mama said. "We're safe at home now, but I still need you to be strong."

Caroline wiped her eyes. "I'll do better when Papa comes home," she promised.

Mama looked out the window for a long moment. Then she said, "Caroline, we both must accept the fact that Papa may still be gone for a long time. We've done all we can do to help him. Now we must do our best to get along without him."

Caroline whispered, "I—I just wish Lieutenant Hathaway wouldn't visit anymore." It hurt her heart to see someone else's father in the kitchen.

"I know it's hard," Mama said. "But you're almost ten now. You're growing into a young woman. I hope you'll find the courage to be a friend to Rhonda." Mama kissed Caroline's forehead. Then she left her alone.

I'll apologize to Rhonda after Papa comes home,

Caroline thought stubbornly. It would be easier to forgive Rhonda's rude comments when Papa was sitting in his own kitchen. In the meantime, though, she would obey Mama and try to be more friendly.

Caroline didn't feel ready to go downstairs. Instead she went to the sewing box Papa had given her and pulled out a piece of the blue cloth she was using to sew her new dress. She was determined to finish it in time for her birthday. She still wished she could make it fancy with lace, but the color was beautiful.

Surely Papa will come in time for my birthday dinner, she thought. She wanted to wear her new dress. She wanted him to see that she was, as Mama had said, becoming a young lady.

Caroline jumped as something pushed against her leg. "Inkpot!" she cried. She put the blue cloth away and scooped the black cat into her arms. He stopped purring long enough to rub his head against her chin.

Caroline settled back on the bed. "We'll *both* be glad to see Papa come home," she murmured. "He'll be here soon now, I think. Very soon."

The next morning, Caroline waited until she saw Rhonda slip outside to fetch water. Caroline grabbed her own shawl and hurried after her. The rain had stopped, but gloomy clouds still hung low in the sky.

She joined Rhonda at the well. "I . . . that is, would you like some help?" Caroline asked politely.

"That would be nice," Rhonda said, just as politely.

The girls worked together to fill two buckets. Then they stood, as if neither one knew what to say. A crow landed on the fence to inspect what was left of the garden. Finally Caroline said, "Let's take these buckets into the kitchen."

For the rest of that day, Caroline and Rhonda didn't argue. They both helped Grandmother with chores and never got cross with each other. But they didn't laugh together or share stories. Caroline thought the icy politeness felt almost as bad as arguing did.

As the days passed, Caroline wished that she knew how to make friends with Rhonda. Oliver had joined the navy, so he wasn't at the house very often. Seth still spent most of his time traveling and delivering mail. Inkpot was a comfort. Grandmother kept Caroline busy. But Caroline still felt hollow inside.

Every day, she watched for her father. When she visited the shipyard, she walked down to the dock, searching the harbor in case he'd escaped and found a canoe or gotten a ride on someone's boat. At home, she watched the lane for a tired traveler. *Everything will be better when Papa gets home*, Caroline thought over and over.

One week crawled by. Then another. Uncle Aaron, Aunt Martha, and Lydia arrived safely from Upper Canada and received a joyful welcome from Oliver, Caroline, and Mama.

Two days later, Caroline's birthday arrived, frosty and clear. But Papa had not come home.

Caroline had just wriggled into her new blue dress that afternoon when Rhonda knocked on the bedroom door. She looked uncertain. Caroline felt uncertain, too. And very, very sad.

"Excuse me," Rhonda said. She met Caroline's

gaze and then quickly looked away. "If you wish, I'd be glad to arrange your hair for you."

"Like yours?" Caroline asked. Rhonda's hairstyle *did* make her look grown-up. "All right."

Rhonda stood behind Caroline and picked up the hairbrush. "Your new dress is pretty."

"It's not as fine as yours," Caroline said with a little shrug.

Rhonda sighed. "Mama says we have to wear nice clothes because Papa is an officer. I wish I didn't have to worry about getting my dress dirty all the time. You're lucky—you have a nice dress *and* one that's easy to work in."

Caroline blinked in surprise. She'd never thought about it that way. She couldn't see Rhonda's face, which made it easier for her to say, "I'm sorry we quarreled that morning in the shipyard."

"I am, too," Rhonda said quickly. "I didn't mean to hurt your feelings."

"And I didn't mean to hurt yours," Caroline said. "I just miss my papa so *much*."

Rhonda took several brushstrokes before saying, "It sounds as if you spent a lot of time together before he was captured."

"My papa and I both love sailing on Lake Ontario better than anything else in the world," Caroline said. "Sometimes I went to the shipyard with him, too."

Rhonda began twisting Caroline's hair into a knot. "My father loves being in the army best," she said. "Mother and Amelia and I follow him from place to place." She picked up a hairpin. "I think... well, I think I felt jealous of you. Knowing that you and your father were sailing together before he was captured made me envious. My father never does anything like that with me."

Rhonda was envious of *her*? Caroline thought about that.

"And if something happened to my father," Rhonda added, "I don't think any of his army friends would look out for us the way Mr. Tate looks after you and your mother."

"Oh," Caroline said in a small voice.

"There," Rhonda said. "I'm finished."

Caroline picked up the small hand mirror on her dresser and caught her breath. She looked so grown-up! "Why, I almost don't recognize myself—but it's pretty. I look like a young lady. Thank you, Rhonda."

Caroline picked up the small hand mirror and caught her breath.
She looked so grown-up!

"You're welcome." Rhonda smiled. "It sounds as if everyone is gathering. Shall we go downstairs?"

✦

For the first time in months, Mama had set the table in the dining room. Caroline hesitated in the doorway. She'd been dreading this moment. If Papa came home right this minute and found a party under way, would he think she'd forgotten him? For a few seconds, Caroline felt frozen.

Then she looked at her family and friends gathered around the table. Uncle Aaron, Aunt Martha, Lydia, and Oliver looked happier than Caroline could remember. Mr. Tate had worn his best clothes. The Hathaways' pretty dresses were like an indoor rainbow of blue, green, and yellow. Seth didn't have a fine shirt to change into, but he'd clearly scrubbed up as best he could. His hair was combed away from his face, and his grin came from the heart.

All these people want to help celebrate my birthday, Caroline thought. A warm feeling slowly filled the frozen place inside.

When everyone was seated, one chair remained

72

empty. "Mama?" Caroline asked. "Is someone else coming?"

"I thought we'd leave an extra chair," Mama said. "Whenever Papa does comes home, it will be waiting."

"I like that idea," Caroline said. "I like it very much."

Mama and Grandmother had prepared a feast: stuffed whitefish, lima beans, cabbage and apples, carrot pudding, and *two* desserts—an apple pie and a burnt-sugar cake.

After the plates had been cleared away, Caroline received several gifts. Grandmother gave her a tin biscuit cutter. Mama gave her a tiny pair of sharp scissors, perfect for snipping embroidery thread.

"And this is from me," Rhonda said. She passed Caroline a handkerchief folded around something small and delicate.

"Oh!" Caroline said, feeling surprised. She hadn't expected a gift from Rhonda. Caroline opened the handkerchief and held up a long piece of lace. "It's so pretty!"

"I made it myself," Rhonda told her shyly. "It's not nearly as fancy as what you might have purchased in Kingston."

Suddenly, Caroline didn't care a bit about fancy lace from Kingston. "It will be perfect on my new dress," she assured Rhonda. "Just perfect." She studied the delicate loops of white cotton thread. "I can't *imagine* how you made this."

"I could show you," Rhonda offered. "All you do is use the little shuttle to make rows of knots, which form those loops."

"Really?" Caroline's eyes went wide with surprise. "I'm good at tying knots!" She and Rhonda exchanged a smile. A real smile this time.

"Speaking of knots," Mr. Tate began, and then he stopped to clear his throat. "Miss Caroline, I don't have a package to give you," he said. "I thought... Well, do you know how to make a French hitch knot?"

Caroline shook her head. "No."

He beamed. "Well, young miss, I'm going to teach you. Once you've learned that knot, I'll help you make the prettiest cider-jug cover you ever saw. Since the jug in your papa's office isn't covered, it could easily get nicked or broken. We'll make a nice cover, and he'll see it as soon as he returns."

Caroline jumped up so fast, her chair almost fell over. She ran around the table and hugged Mr. Tate. "What a wonderful gift," she said. "Thank you."

Caroline thought that was the last present, but after she'd settled back in her place, Aunt Martha came around the table and handed her a parcel. "This isn't really from us," she said, exchanging a glance with Uncle Aaron and Lydia. "We're just delivering it."

Puzzled, Caroline pulled away the cloth wrapping and found a wooden box. The lid was decorated with tiny bits of golden straw that had been pasted into fancy designs around the edge. Darker pieces of straw spelled out *CAROLINE.*

"I can keep my embroidery silks in here," Caroline said, turning the delicate box in her hands. "But . . . who made it?"

Aunt Martha smiled. "All we know for *certain* is that it was waiting on our doorstep one morning, right before we left Upper Canada."

Caroline gasped. "It's from Papa!" She remembered seeing scraps of wood in his room at Point Frederick, and his mattress had been stuffed with straw. "But how did he get it to you?"

Uncle Aaron spread his hands. "We don't know! There was no note. Putting anything in writing was likely too dangerous. But we think one of the guards at the fort brought it to us as a favor to your father."

Caroline gently touched the box with one finger. Her heart had been filled with anger and hatred toward the British. It was hard to take in this new idea, that one of them had done such a kindness. She suddenly remembered the guard with the scar on his cheek who had whispered after her on the stairs, *Your father misses you.*

Tears filled Caroline's eyes. One spilled down her cheek before she could wipe it away. "Excuse me," she said, pushing back her chair. She hurried into the kitchen, scooped Inkpot from the rug by the hearth, and held him close. He began to purr.

Grandmother followed her into the room, leaning heavily on her cane. "Caroline? What's wrong?"

"Everyone has been so kind to me," Caroline began. "Even a British soldier!"

Grandmother raised her eyebrows, waiting for Caroline to continue.

"It doesn't seem fair to Papa to feel happy and to celebrate..." Caroline's voice trailed away. It was

76

hard to explain her tangled feelings.

Grandmother regarded her. "What do you think your papa would say if he were here?"

"Well," Caroline said slowly, "I don't think he'd want me to be unhappy."

"I *know* he wouldn't," Grandmother said firmly. "You're holding him in your heart, Caroline. That's what matters."

Caroline considered that idea, studying it like a new color of silk to be stitched into a picture. "I think you're right," she admitted finally. "But Grandmother? I'll never stop hoping. Never stop waiting for Papa to come home."

"Of course not," Grandmother said. "None of us will."

Caroline heard the murmur of conversation from the next room, where people she loved had gathered to honor her birthday. She reached for her grandmother's hand. "Come along," she said. "Let's go back to the party."

LOOKING BACK

WARTIME
IN
1812

In the early 1800s, Americans depended on shipping to get supplies and to keep their businesses running.

The War of 1812 is sometimes called "the war that almost no one wanted." Many people living in New York, Caroline's home state, were opposed to the war. So were people in Connecticut, Rhode Island, Massachusetts, and other New England states. They wanted the United States to settle its differences with England peacefully.

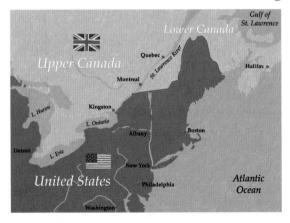

People living along the coast and Great Lakes feared that war would hurt the shipping trade.

Looking at a map from Caroline's time, it's easy to see why. The people most opposed to the war lived along the Atlantic Ocean or the great inland water-ways—Lake Erie, Lake Ontario, and the Saint Lawrence River, which

80

connects the Great Lakes to the Atlantic. If British ships blocked ports, then food and other supplies could not be delivered. Businesses in these regions depended on being able to send and receive goods by ship. With the United States and Britain battling for control of the waterways, shipping became more dangerous and difficult than ever.

Attacking soldiers sometimes searched people's homes, stealing food and belongings.

For families like Caroline's, the war was a storm that left almost no part of life undisturbed. Simply having American troops marching nearby could turn people's lives upside down, because the army sometimes took over their barns and even their homes so that soldiers would have a place

to sleep. People were even more terrified when enemy ships and troops came near. If a battle broke out, women and children living nearby often ran for their lives.

Families fleeing into the woods to escape a battle

War tore apart families and friendships, too. Before war broke out, many Americans had friends and relatives in Upper Canada, and they often went there to visit or do business. Once the war began, some of those friends and relatives sided with the British and became enemies.

Americans could look across the Saint Lawrence River and see the British colony of Upper Canada.

The war also separated wives from their husbands and children from their fathers. When war was declared, soldiers, sailors, marines, and army officers like Rhonda's father were called to duty. But in 1812, the U.S. Army and

On both sides, families said sad good-byes as husbands and fathers marched off to war.

Navy were much smaller than Britain's. The army began offering cash bonuses and free land to encourage men to join. Many men and boys, some as young as 14 or 15 years old, signed up.

Other men joined volunteer militia, ready to fight if the enemy came near. When an attack seemed likely, signal guns rang out and riders raced on horseback through the countryside, alerting the militiamen to leave their homes and fight.

A rider spreading the news that the enemy is near

Some men, like Caroline's father, had no chance to fight. They were captured by the British and held on ships or in Canadian prisons for months or even years.

Who would do the work that the men had left

behind? It was up to women and children. During Caroline's time, most women already worked very hard. They needed to be skilled and physically strong to keep their homes and families going. Women spun yarn and thread, wove cloth, sewed clothing, and made soap and candles.

Women and girls sewed nearly all the clothing for their family and kept it neatly mended.

They grew and preserved food for their families. When war came, women had to work even harder. They had to use their skills to keep their husbands' businesses going, too. Like Mrs. Abbott, who took over the management of her husband's shipyard, many women managed their families' stores, inns, taverns, farms, and leather tanneries. Women kept blacksmith forges blazing and printing presses running.

A woman carrying grain from the field

Some women didn't stop there. Like Caroline's mother, women made daring trips into enemy territory to buy or beg for the release of their husbands or sons from prison. Other women rolled up their sleeves and joined in the fighting. Fanny Doyle was the wife of an American soldier who helped fire a cannon at Fort Niagara, New York. When her husband was captured during a fierce battle, she bravely took his place in the fighting.

New Yorker Fanny Doyle bravely fought in battle.

Enemy cannonballs fell around her like rain. Still, she stood her ground, loading cannons until the battle ended.

This map sampler was stitched by a girl in 1809.

During Caroline's time, most people worked with their hands. Even in troubled times, people put effort and skill into the things they crafted by hand. After girls were done with the day's chores, they stitched *samplers*—squares of linen or silk decorated with colorful thread. Working on samplers was more than just a way to practice making the tiny, careful stitches they would need for sewing clothes. By stitching the alphabet, multiplication tables, and maps into their samplers, girls were practicing their reading, arithmetic, and geography, too. Perhaps many girls also felt as Caroline did—that their hearts would stay lighter if their minds and hands stayed busy.

Even men held in enemy prisons found ways to work with their hands. Prisoners like Caroline's father passed time in their cells by collecting tiny bits of straw, bone, or wood and piecing them together. The imaginative boxes, toys, and tiny model ships they created show that even as war was destroying people's homes and lives, it did not destroy their hope. Not even war could stop them from trying to put things together in ways that were both useful and beautiful.

This handmade box from Caroline's time is decorated with inlaid bits of straw.

A SNEAK PEEK AT

A SURPRISE FOR

Caroline

When Lydia and Rhonda become friends, Caroline feels left out. Will Christmas gifts and winter fun mend Caroline's friendships—or push the girls farther apart?

That night Caroline lay in bed, listening to the two older girls whisper together from their pallets on the floor nearby. *Perhaps I should forget all about skating,* Caroline thought miserably.

But that didn't feel like a good solution. Caroline considered what Rhonda had said earlier about skating. Perhaps Rhonda was still afraid of falling. Caroline wished she'd taken the time to explain her tow-rope plan when she'd presented the skates to Rhonda. Surely that would have put Rhonda's fears to rest! Before finally drifting off to sleep, Caroline knew what she needed to do.

The morning after Christmas dawned clear and cold. After breakfast, Caroline found Lydia and Rhonda in the parlor. "Mama has excused us from lessons today," Caroline began. "And it's a perfect morning for skating." Before Rhonda could protest, Caroline quickly explained her idea.

"You want to tow Rhonda over the ice?" Lydia repeated thoughtfully. "That just might work. Getting started is the hardest part of learning to skate."

Rhonda twisted her fingers together. "I don't know."

Lydia looked from her cousin to her friend.

"Skating really is great fun," she said. "With a little practice, you'll be ready to glide all over the ice."

"And if you give skating a fair try, I'll do whatever you'd like to do afterward," Caroline promised.

"Oh, very well," Rhonda said reluctantly. "I'll try."

The girls dressed in their warmest clothes, gathered up their skates, and headed down to the harbor. Lots of other people were already skating on the frozen lake—some hesitant, others with great speed and grace. A few skated near the navy ships, but Caroline didn't want to go there. Sailors had chopped trenches in the ice around their vessels so spies or enemy soldiers couldn't walk across the frozen lake and sneak aboard. Caroline didn't want to take Rhonda anywhere near open water!

"Let's go over there," she said, pointing to an area that was well away from the ships and most of the other skaters.

"Are you sure the ice is safe?" Rhonda asked.

"Yes," Caroline said firmly. "Bad ice looks dark. This thick ice has a nice white color. See?"

Rhonda watched a man and woman using a

chair sled nearby. The man was skating and pushing his sweetheart along while she sat on the sled. "They look a lot heavier than we are," she said, "and the ice is holding them up."

"I've seen horse-drawn sleighs pass through here, too," Lydia assured her.

Rhonda squared her shoulders. "All right, then. I'm ready."

Caroline and Lydia strapped on their own skates and helped Rhonda put on hers. "Before you start skating, watch how I do it," Caroline told her friend. She pushed off on the ice. With just a few strokes, she felt as if she were flying! It was wonderful to glide over the frozen lake.

Before going too far, though, she remembered why she and her friends had come. Reluctantly she slowed and returned to the shore. "See?" she said to Rhonda. "You'll soon be gliding like that too."

While Lydia tied one end of the rope she'd borrowed from the shipyard around Rhonda's waist, Caroline knotted the other end around her own. Caroline and Lydia helped Rhonda stand, and then they slowly moved onto the ice.

"My ankles are shaking already!" Rhonda cried.

Caroline pushed off on the ice. With just a few strokes,
she felt as if she were flying!

"Hold on to my arm," Lydia said. "Caroline, start pulling!"

Caroline pushed off on one foot. "Ooh!" she gasped, as the tow rope tightened around her waist. Pulling Rhonda was more difficult than she'd expected.

She wasn't about to give up, though. She dug the tip of one skate into the ice and shoved off harder. That sent her forward a few inches. She pushed off again with her other foot.

"Faster!" Lydia urged.

I'm trying! Caroline thought. Summoning every bit of her strength, she kept skating forward. They all began to move a little more quickly.

"That's the way," Lydia called.

Caroline clenched her teeth and chanted silently, *Push off with the left foot, push off with the right.* Even this solid ice had bumps and tiny cracks, but she tried to avoid them. Finally she picked up enough speed that it became a little easier to keep skating.

"I'm doing it!" Rhonda exclaimed. "I'm really skating!"

Rhonda sounded so happy that Caroline dared a look over her shoulder. Rhonda was taking little strokes herself. "Isn't this fun?" Caroline called. Rhonda nodded.

Caroline looked ahead again—and saw a ridge in the ice, right in front of her. She gave a little hop, easily clearing the rough spot, but she knew Rhonda wasn't ready to make such a move.

"Watch out!" Caroline yelled.

READ ALL OF CAROLINE'S STORIES,
available at bookstores and *americangirl.com.*

MEET CAROLINE
When the British attack Caroline's village, she
makes a daring choice that helps to win the day.

CAROLINE'S SECRET MESSAGE
Caroline and Mama take a dangerous journey
to the British fort where Papa is held prisoner.

A SURPRISE FOR CAROLINE
Caroline finds herself on thin ice after
friendship troubles lead to a bad decision.

CAROLINE TAKES A CHANCE
When a warship threatens American supplies,
can Caroline's little fishing boat turn it away?

CAROLINE'S BATTLE
As a battle rages right in her own village,
Caroline faces a terrible choice.

CHANGES FOR CAROLINE
Caroline pitches in on her cousin's new farm—
and comes home to a wonderful surprise.